To Dave,
Enjoy!
Think of Banff!

The Transported Faun

Cassy Welburn

Cassy Welburn with Al Cairns

The Transported Faun

Radical Bookshop and Press
4838 Richard Road SW, Suite 300
Calgary, AB T3E 6L1

FIC029000 - Fiction, Short Stories

Chinook Blast Collection
Volume 1
February 1, 2021

Editors: Lexie Angelo
Cover Design: Lexie Angelo

ISBN-13: 978-1-990201-09-7

Printed in the United States

Typeset in Capitolina

To A.T.J. Cairns, my late husband

Oxford Scholar and English professor at the University of Calgary, 1962-1988

contents

The Transported Faun

I call it the blink of nature.

It can take you by surprise when you return, say, to a favourite camping spot, or, in my case, a hiking trail in the mountains, after a long absence. I had felt it before when returning to the lookout tower after a winter in the city. That whiff of disbelief—a shaking of the head—of the trees themselves. As though they won't part for me to pass. My return this time was no different except that I'd been gone longer. It must be forty years since I last climbed this trail. Forty years since I've even thought of coming back to the mountain. But this time I had an awareness of something watching, weighing and even testing me. A scent of decay in the air like a half- forgotten memory.

I had heard that fires had worsened in the Rockies since my youthful days on the tower, when we scanned the horizon and reported in on the hour. Electronic monitoring has long since replaced all that climbing with binoculars in hand. It wasn't the familiar smell of smoke I felt through my skin, but a kind of musk as thick and damp as fog.

I sensed a cautiousness that lasted some time, and then, acceptance. Something was watching me, but it wasn't a person—human eyes have a more familiar feel. An animal didn't seem right either. Animals here in the National Park are not shy, though they, too, seem altered in some way. And they don't watch a person for days, at the same place, at the same hour.

I found a viewpoint—one I'd never come across in the past—and I returned for a few hours each day to sit and eat my lunch. The view was a short drive from my room in Banff, followed by a hike up Tunnel Mountain. I was lucky that the trailhead was open to hikers unlike many others in the park. The park officials weren't taking any chances with bears or fire this summer, of all the summers I had decided to return.

A clearing near the flat limestone slabs at the top of the curve was circled by narrow dark-green pines where a glimpse of the surrounding peaks could just be seen above the timberline. The towering branches of a colossal lodge pole pine hid the entrance to what could have been a cave; a promise of cool in all this blistering heat.

There was an Arcadian beauty about the place that reminded me of the ancient sites where temples were built into caves and altars from angled stones. I thought of Europe, where I'd led so many tours of graduate students, and hoped to again, after my retirement. It's hard to believe that life has been closed to me, now, after a student went missing. The student had left the tour earlier and I was not found responsible. But I could not get it out of my head. How I might have misled someone with a word, a missed call or a simple lack of response and they vanished. How no amount of looking could bring them back.

This mountain, at least, is real. My past here is a history I can hold in my mind. But there are details I don't remember, like a glacial stream or a spring leaping from the rocks. How could I have forgotten about this place all these years?

Still, I was being watched. It felt like a boyhood game I had once played. If I turned suddenly, I could almost catch a glimpse of a movement. But I didn't feel fear, only the return of what I call archaic joy.

There must be a reason, I thought—something nagging at me that needed to be remembered—or a new possibility that wanted to be known. Something beyond the academic life I'd embraced for so long, but which now had released me. "Take some time," they had said but I began to suspect that time was going to be longer than planned. Each day that I stayed the dread of waking up to my present reality faded a little, and I felt an unexpected childhood begin to grow.

Then he appeared.

I had heard of fauns and seen their marble statues in museums in Greece. I'd often wondered if they'd survived somehow, retreated to wilder, but more hidden places, where someone could look after them.

This is not where I'd expect to find a faun. In the Mediterranean maybe, but not here. Unless someone had brought him. From the first, 'him' rather than 'it' seemed natural. Also, I began to sense the faun was ill—in body or in spirit I couldn't tell. He looked like a faun should look—a lean face, no beard, and thick curly hair, grey at the temples, from which barely protruded two small, blunt horns. His torso, though, was covered to the haunches by a long woollen garment reaching past two hairy goat's legs to their cloven hooves. He was cold, in spite of the heat.

The faun was shy at first, not wanting to make eye contact (his pupils were elongated like a goat's, but with a warmer expression), he held out a small hand. "Hello—."

I took his hand, a gentle grip, and felt the palm covered in hair.

"How are you?" I asked.

"Very well... I am very well," the faun said. His voice was high with a liquid accent. "And you?"

"I am well." I was unsure of how much English he understood. I opened my pack to share my lunch. "Can we sit here?" I stretched out on the grass. He accepted, squatting to eat. He even drank my wine with delight.

"Ah—I knew you would be—what is the word—sympathetic." He ate an orange through the peel, biting into it with sharp, white teeth. "Wine and bread, food of the gods," he said smiling. "Ah... and fruit." He then removed the meat from the bread and tossed it away. "A cold sun," he muttered, the ageless face dark suddenly with weariness. "Would you like to see where I live? It is not very far...."

"Very much. If you don't mind?"

"We are like your cats, 'independent,' is that your word? It is not really possible for me to go into town. Sometimes, I talk to children. They tell their parents, but of course no one believes them. We like the silent places, but we do not really like to be alone."

I sensed his isolation; had he also sensed mine? Different solitudes of course, but neither of us, had become what we were by choice.

The faun led me to the cave I had noticed earlier, with the entrance carefully disguised. It was clean and simply furnished; the floor swept with a twig broom and a straw mattress placed in one corner. He led me to a garden down by the stream, with vegetables growing in profusion in spite of the dry summer heat. I began to relax, sitting on a log in the garden, in a way I had not been able to for years. The wind swirled a gust of birds high into the air against the pines and the peak of mountain rising above them, a holy breath on my skin. We didn't speak, just sat in the sun side by side, the faun occasionally glancing my way with only the hint of a smile.

Elk had gathered outside my window while I slept. Their rustling and chewing sounds had broken through my dreams. I only half-remembered coming back to my hotel, the night another hole in my rapidly decreasing past. I arose and stuffed all the food I had bought into my backpack, along with extra clothing. The hotel clerk called to remind me about checking out as they were closing early for the season, but I was already getting into the car.

I returned to the trailhead where I saw yellow barrier ribbons strung across the trees when I climbed up the path from the parking lot. I was not out of breath but swung my arms effortlessly. I used to run up this trail, and the memory pouring back spurred me on. The dry, hot air caught at my throat, but did not slow me down.

"You are here," I said. "I wasn't sure if I'd dreamt it all."

"I knew you would return," the faun said, holding out his hand. "In my home in Greece there was no sense of time," he pulled me up onto his pathway, smiling now so his whole face shone, "until the change came that altered my family."

We walked together around the side of the mountain. "The family had always looked after me," he said. "Each village used to have a faun then, and everyone shared in its care. They shared, too, in the bounty of the wild areas it watched over. But we each belonged to only one chosen family. The family would come into the woods or bring me into their own house. I brought the sounds of merriment to the woods and even to their homes."

13

I had a hard time keeping up to him as he strode ahead. I called after him, "Where are you taking me?" But he had become excited with no one to speak to for so long. Now he could not stop. We stood at the edge of the cliff—one of the 'viewpoints' officially labelled the forest and wildlife that could be seen. There were no people about. I thought for a fleeting moment how easy it would be to capture his picture, a new wildlife not yet identified.

"Then the family lost its land," he went on. "They were told they had never owned it and their grove of trees was to be cut down for a new development. There was nothing they could do but come here, with the help of relatives who sent them the money. In the end, they could not leave me behind. It was a selfish act. They knew the whole village would be affected, and the wood beyond." The faun sat down on a rock, his feet clattering loose stones that began to tumble and bounce down the side of the cliff, touching the toes of my boots. I realized that my camera had slipped from my hand, refusing to take this last thing, his image, from him.

"They didn't even tell me," he shouted as if to the trees. "It was the time of my hibernation and I was simply 'crated', like furniture, across the sea. The villagers knew nothing. I belonged to all of them as well as to my family. I fell asleep in my cave and awoke—here in Canada. I was surprised of course, even alarmed, but I adjusted, as well as any animal can. We were very close at first—the bond of strangers in a strange land. I could always hear Greek spoken then. Gradually, this too changed. They began to speak English for their children, and now the grandchildren don't know the language at all."

"Did they take you around with them?" I asked as we started to turn back, climbing up the rocky slope toward his home. "Did you ride in the car, speak to people? How did they explain you?"

14

He laughed and waved a hand at the hoodoos in the distance, where a few hikers were taking pictures. "Not here, no, I wasn't allowed out. They started to hide me in the basement—me, so used to the woods and trees. Then, as their restaurant grew, I became the dishwasher. Me! The children became ashamed to bring their friends home, and I was forever being hidden. I came out here," he gestured at the view, as though somehow I was repellent, "and here I came to stay. I don't like to bother them now. I'm just a childish memory." The faun left me then as we reached the cave, retreating inside as though he had forgotten I was there.

I sat down under a pine, his story ringing in my head, mixing and binding with all the others I had tried so hard to keep straight. I leaned against the tree until the heat became unbearable and its branches pressed into my back painfully. Finally, I went into the cave, wrapped myself in a blanket and let the cool air engulf me.

"I've made a drink for you," the faun said as he held a glass out for me. I reached for it and took a sip. It was a light, lucent golden colour—almost like sunlight. It was different from any I'd had before, intoxicating without dimming or distorting. It heightened my awareness without falsifying it. He called it Ambrosia, apologizing for its qualities.

"It's not quite as it should be," he said. "Not all the ingredients are available. It is a very old formula."

"The drink of the Olympians," I said, lifting my glass to finish, in what felt like an awkward ceremony. "Will it make me immortal?"

"Sometimes I wonder if even I exist any longer," he said, his voice thin. "These are not my woods and not my world. As long as the old people were still alive, there was something. But my family died; the father ten years ago, the mother seven. The children—they are busy with their business. And their children—I do not think they ever believed. Everywhere now there is a lack of imagination. Anyway, they prosper, and I do not wish to disturb their reality." He was silent for a few moments, the sun throwing everything into sharp, shadowed relief. "I have retreated to the edges and waited. I thought my family would in time return, but I did not foresee this, and it will not pass."

"What won't pass?" I put a hand to my head to steady myself, feeling the air thicken with smoke.

The faun had drifted into a half sleep, into a barely audible, almost oracular distance. "The winds, the trees, even here, they need me, ask too much of me," he said. "They ask me to make music."

Outside the cave a small herd of elk had gathered, their restlessness disturbing the air. The sun now a pulsing, red smear behind the mist that was becoming omnipresent.

"They have always been wary of me," the faun shrugged. "Men, because too much of me is animal; animals because too much of me is man. I know what they know. Something is coming—is partly already here—and they are afraid, and I am too." His eyes had darkened—the elongated pupils shining a dark gold.

The elk had come closer. I hadn't heard the bugling of a bull elk in a long time. The sound sent me back to my first summer in the tower when I watched as down below two elk charged each other. I heard the crash of their antlers and their grunts. All morning they charged, bawling and fighting in the sharp autumn air. I thought the struggle would never end, and that neither one would subside. I would be preserved there in my tower forever listening.

Then that morning splintered. A crow's sharp cry, plaintive and lingering in the dead air, brought me back. The elk stood

16

patiently. A fine silt of ash drifted down on us. Outside the cave I could hear the wind start up again, from the west this time. "I should go—I need to find my car," I said, but the faun didn't move. He seemed shrunken, fading into himself. "I'll come back." I said, "I'll bring the car and take you with me. We can find a place together."

I staggered out of the cave and down to the end of the switchbacks before I heard it. On the highway a car horn blared. Then the din of more horns sounded. Through the wind's steady hum came the rustling and shuffling of many feet. Animals were leaving. Sheep, mountain goats, elk rushed past the cars, enveloped in a smoky film that filled my lungs before I could wrap a shirt around my face. Would I be able to find my car in all this? There was nothing more of myself I could retrieve. Animal eyes followed me, and their limbs scraped mine, forcing the breath from my body. I couldn't get it straight anymore, couldn't arrange memories in their correct order. I was here, I told myself, back on my mountain, and that was all that mattered.

The trees thinned further up the mountain, rooted in a rocky and barren ridge. I thought I had made a wrong turn for a moment. I was disoriented by the animals following me so closely, stopping when I stopped. Then I saw the clothes thrown out by the cave's entrance and a pot on the dry grass. When I looked inside, I saw the faun face down on the floor and dead. I knew before I turned him over.

I found a small shovel though it was dark, and buried him there just outside the cave, the sting of the wind in my face the whole time. The soil flew back at me, the shovel slipping through my hands. All the while, the goats beside me were pushing and creeping closer. I thought I saw a cougar go by, so quietly, gone before I could quite make it out. Calmness settled over me then. I was in my cave and down below, Banff was burning.

How long I had been standing there, I don't know. I don't mark the days off like I did on the tower that once stood in this very place. The town below has changed. There are pieces missing that I will never find or put together. Still, on the turnout below where they advertise the animals that can be found here, I sensed someone watching. A man with binoculars. If I turned suddenly, he could almost catch a glimpse of me.

ACKNOWLEDGEMENTS

I would like to acknowledge Al Cairns for his writing about Banff, from which I was inspired to adapt this story.

ABOUT THE AUTHOR

Cassy Welburn is a Calgary writer and storyteller whose work has appeared in journals across Canada and on CBC radio. Her book of poetry, Changelings, with CD-Cassiopeia, came out with Frontenac House, 2015.

SPECIAL THANKS

Chinook Blast Festival

The City of Calgary

Tourism Calgary

Calgary Municipal Land Corporation

Calgary Arts Development

Calgary Public Library

IngramSpark

CPSIA information can be obtained
at www.ICGtesting.com
Printed in the USA
BVHW082027230221
600842BV00001B/104